A New Home in Space

by Damian Harvey and José Rubert

W
FRANKLIN WATTS

Chapter 1

"Look!" said Dad, pointing through the window of the space shuttle. "There it is. Our new home in space."

Theo let out a little gasp as New Earth came into view. It was huge ... even bigger than he had imagined.

New Earth was the biggest space station in the galaxy. It had shops and cinemas, libraries and hospitals. It even had parks and schools. Mum and Dad said it would be the perfect place to live and work.

Theo wasn't so sure. While Mum and Dad
were starting their new job, he would be going to
a new school. It wasn't the first time Theo
had moved to a new school, but this would be
different. He'd never even been on
a space station before.
Dad said there was nothing to worry about,
and that it would be just like living on planet Earth.

But Theo couldn't help worrying.

He worried about what the people would be like.

He worried about fitting in and making new friends.

As the space shuttle landed, Mum smiled.

"Isn't it exciting?" she said.

Theo didn't feel excited at all,

but he tried his best to smile.

Chapter 2

The next morning, Theo was eating breakfast
when there was a knock at the door.

"Hurry up!" said Mum. "Leni's here."

Leni lived next door and went to the same school
as Theo. "Come on," said Leni. "You don't want to
be late on your first day."

As they walked, Theo asked, "What time does
the bus arrive?"

Leni frowned. "What's a bus?" she said.

Now it was Theo's turn to frown.

"The thing that takes us to school," he said.

"We don't have buses," said Leni. "We have pods.

Look, here's ours now."

Theo stared at the pod in amazement.
It looked like a large glass egg with
school children sitting inside it.

Inside the pod, Theo tried to relax and enjoy
the ride. But then, a little way ahead of them,
Theo spotted a large hole in the floor.
Their pod was heading straight for it.
"Look out!" cried Theo. "We're going to crash."

But instead of crashing, the pod went gently down into the hole to another level of the space station. The other children laughed and Theo felt his face turning bright red.

"Don't worry," smiled Leni. "Everyone is worried the first time they ride in a pod. You'll get used to it."

Theo shook his head. He didn't think he'd ever get used to it.

Chapter 3

Theo's new school was a maze of walkways and moving platforms. By the time they reached their classroom, he felt completely lost.

As Miss Chang took the register, Theo looked around at the other children. He recognised some from the ride in the pod and remembered how silly he'd felt.

He wondered what the class would be doing today and hoped he wouldn't embarrass himself again.

When Miss Chang announced they would be playing gravity ball, everyone cheered and started chatting excitedly. Theo hadn't heard of gravity ball but at his old school he'd been good at sports. He was sure gravity ball would be easy … but he was wrong.

The other children floated around the room, passing the ball to each other and scoring goals. Theo just bobbed in the air like a balloon.

"This is impossible," complained Theo.

"Try pushing off against the walls," said Leni,

"then keep moving."

Theo tried what Leni suggested but it was no use.

He couldn't even get close to the ball.

Theo was ready to give up when the ball bounced

off his head and floated into the goal. It had only

been luck, but Theo grinned as everyone cheered.

Chapter 4

At lunchtime, Theo sat with Leni and other children
from their class. They talked about gravity ball.
Theo discovered that everyone found it difficult
at first.

"I spent my first lesson floating upside down,"
said Zack.

"That's nothing!" confessed Kali. "I got stuck in
the goal."

Everyone laughed as they shared their gravity ball
disaster stories.

"Perhaps this won't be so bad after all,"
thought Theo.

After lunch, the class learnt about different jobs people did on the space station. Then Miss Chang said she'd had a good idea.

"We can all tell everyone about our parents' jobs," she said. "It will be interesting and will help Theo feel more at home."

At first, Theo thought this sounded like a good idea. But he soon changed his mind.

Zack told everyone his mum was an engineer.

"She's one of the people that keep the space
station running," he said, proudly.

"My dad flies space shuttles," said Leni.

Kali's parents were scientists and Goran's mum
was a doctor.

It seemed like everyone's parents had very important jobs. Theo didn't want to say what his mum and dad did. He was sure the children would all laugh at him.

Luckily, the bell went before it was Theo's turn.

Chapter 5

The next morning, Miss Chang looked at Theo.

"Now, would you like to tell everyone what your parents do?" she asked.

Theo could feel his face turning red.

"Not really, Miss," he replied.

"Go on Theo, don't be shy," said his teacher.

"I can't, Miss," said Theo. "It's top secret!"

There was a surprised gasp from the rest of the class and Theo felt himself turning even redder than before. He thought Miss Chang might tell him off, but she was grinning at him.

"That's right," said Miss Chang. "It's top secret until after lunch. As a special treat, I've asked Theo's mum and dad to come to school today."

Theo groaned. Just when he thought things couldn't get any worse, this happened.

After lunch, everyone followed Miss Chang into the playground.

"This is so embarrassing," said Theo when he saw Mum and Dad in their Galaxy Ices ice-cream van. But to Theo's surprise, everyone cheered.

Then he watched in amazement as they all ran to get an ice cream.

"Why didn't you tell us what your parents did?" cried Zack.

"Your parents have all got cool jobs," said Theo. "I was worried that driving an ice-cream van was too ordinary."

Kali licked her Super Strawberry Fizz Galaxy Ice

and grinned. "Not ordinary at all," she said.

"It's the coolest thing in the galaxy. You're so lucky."

Theo grinned. He was so happy to have made

some new friends. He waited for an ice cream, too.

Things to think about

1. Why do you think Theo is nervous at the beginning of the story?
2. How do you think living in a space station will affect Theo?
3. Have you ever been the new person in school or at a club? How did it feel?
4. Why is Theo so nervous about his new friends finding out about his parents' job?

Write it yourself

One of the themes in this story is making friends.
Now try to write your own story with a similar theme.
Plan your story before you begin to write it.
Start off with a story map:
• a beginning to introduce the characters and where and when your story is set (the setting);
• a problem which the main characters will need to fix in the story;
• an ending where the problems are resolved.

Get writing! Try to use interesting descriptions, such as the simile: "Theo bobbed in the air like a balloon" to describe your story world and excite your reader.

Notes for parents and carers

Independent reading

The aim of independent reading is to read this book with ease. This series is designed to provide an opportunity for your child to read for pleasure and enjoyment. These notes are written for you to help your child make the most of this book.

About the book

In this story, we follow Theo as he joins a new school on board a space station. Everything is very different, and he doesn't feel like he will ever fit in. His nerves are just beginning to settle when the teacher announces that his parents are coming to school. Theo is embarrassed about his parents' job, but his new friends soon help him overcome his worries.

Before reading

Ask your child why they have selected this book. Look at the title and blurb together. What do they think it will be about? Do they think they will like it?

During reading

Encourage your child to read independently. If they get stuck on a longer word, remind them that they can find syllable chunks that can be sounded out from left to right. They can also read on in the sentence and think about what would make sense.

After reading

Support comprehension by talking about the story. What happened?
Then help your child think about the messages in the book that go beyond the story, using the questions on the page opposite.
Give your child a chance to respond to the story, asking:
Did you enjoy the story and why? Who was your favourite character?
What was your favourite part? What did you expect to happen at the end?

Franklin Watts
First published in Great Britain in 2018
by The Watts Publishing Group

Copyright © The Watts Publishing Group 2018
All rights reserved.

Series Editors: Jackie Hamley and Melanie Palmer
Series Advisors: Dr Sue Bodman and Glen Franklin
Series Designer: Peter Scoulding

A CIP catalogue record for this book is
available from the British Library.

ISBN 978 1 4451 6327 7 (hbk)
ISBN 978 1 4451 6329 1 (pbk)
ISBN 978 1 4451 6328 4 (library ebook)

Printed in China

Franklin Watts
An imprint of
Hachette Children's Group
Part of The Watts Publishing Group
Carmelite House
50 Victoria Embankment
London EC4Y 0DZ

An Hachette UK Company
www.hachette.co.uk

www.franklinwatts.co.uk